With a Little Help From
DADDY

Margaret K. McElderry Books

An imprint of Simon & Schuster Children's Publishing Division

1230 Avenue of the Americas, New York, New York 10020

Book design by Ann Bobco

Hand-lettering by Dan Andreasen

The text for this book is set in ITC Officina Serif.

The illustrations for this book are rendered in oil paint.

Manufactured in China

2 4 6 8 10 9 7 5 3 1

Library of Congress Cataloging-in-Publication Data

Andreasen, Dan.

With a little help from Daddy / Dan Andreasen.

p. cm.

Summary: A young boy lists ways in which he is special—the tallest, cutest, fastest boy on
the block—including the one wonderful trait with which his father helps.

ISBN 0-689-84565-0 (hardcover)

[1. Individuality—Fiction. 2. Fathers and sons—Fiction.] I. Title.

PZ7.A55915 Wi 2003

[E]—dc21

2002002694

With a Little Help From

DADDY

by DAN ANDREASEN

Margaret K. McElderry Books

New York   London   Toronto   Sydney   Singapore

*For my father, Kermit,
and my son, Bret*

Look at me!

I'm the tallest boy
on my block.

I'm also the fastest boy
on my block.

And the strongest.

Look what I can do!
One!
Two!

I'm the
smartest boy
on
my block.

On Tuesdays and Saturdays,
   I'm the cleanest boy on my block.

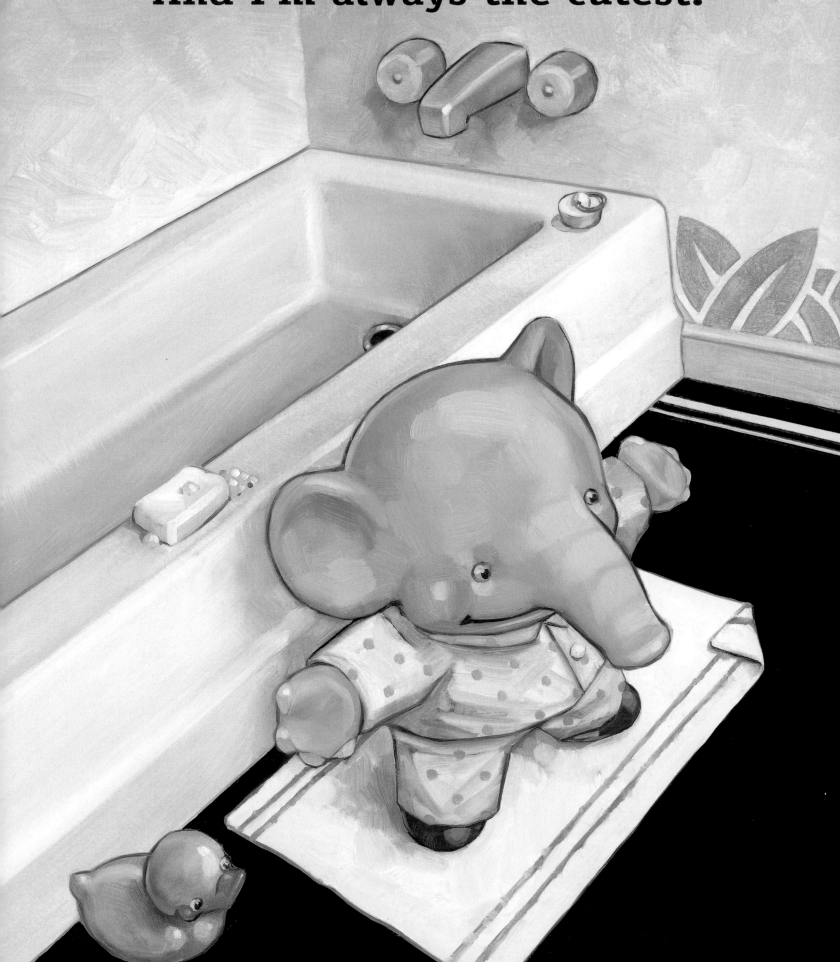

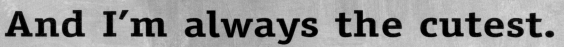

And I'm always the cutest.

When I remember,
I'm the most polite boy
on my block.

And I love being the silliest!

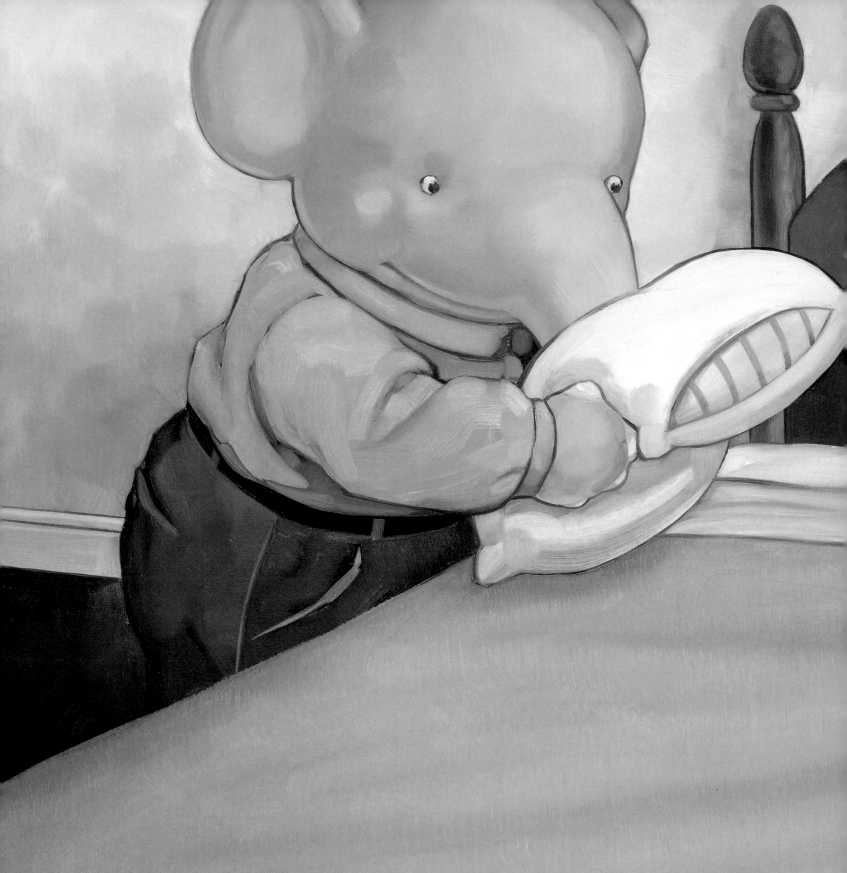

I'm the neatest boy on my block.

I can be the noisiest boy
on my block.

BANG!
BOOM!
CRASH!

**Sometimes I'm the bravest boy
on my block.**

When I cross the street,
I'm the safest boy on my block.

But most of all,
I'm the happiest boy
on my block . . .